WITHDRAWN

Hoggle's Christmas

HOGGLE'S CHRISTMAS

Rick Shelton

Illustrated by
Donald Gates

COBBLEHILL BOOKS/Dutton
New York

Library of Congress Cataloging-in-Publication Data

Shelton, Rick.
Hoggle's Christmas / Rick Shelton ; illustrated by Donald Gates.
          p.   cm.
Summary: A young sister and brother make an unusual friend who
leaves and remembers them with a Christmas surprise.
ISBN 0-525-65129-2
[1. Brothers and sisters—Fiction.   2. Friendship—Fiction.]
I. Gates, Donald, ill.   II. Title.
PZ7.S5416Ho   1993   [Fic]—dc20   92-37861   CIP   AC

Published in the United States by Cobblehill Books,
an affiliate of Dutton Children's Books,
a division of Penguin Books USA Inc.,
375 Hudson Street, New York, New York 10014
Designed by Joy Taylor

Printed in the United States of America
First Edition   10 9 8 7 6 5 4 3 2 1

Contents

CHAPTER 1

▲▲▲▲▲▲▲▲▲▲▲▲▲▲▲▲▲▲▲▲

The Movers

The day Hoggle left, it was very hot. It was one of those late August days in Alabama when the pavement on the street burns right through the bottoms of your shoes. Richard and Isabel Glover stood in Hoggle's front yard watching the movers carry Hoggle's furniture out of his house and load it into a big green and yellow truck.

"I wish Hoggle had taken us with him," Richard said to Isabel.

"Let's call him. We could do that."

"No we can't. We don't even know where he

is. He could be in Iowa or New Jersey. Anyway, wherever he is, he probably has enough to think about."

"Do you think he's thinking about us?" Isabel said.

"Beats me."

"Where's New Jersey, Richard?"

"It's way up north, next to New York."

"Is it in Canada?"

"Almost." Richard picked his bicycle up off the curb. "I'm getting out of here."

The movers were still bringing things out of the house—boxes and lamps and bookcases. The three men looked like professional wrestlers. They had huge hands, wide shoulders, and big stomachs. One of them was named Dave; at least that was what the yellow patch over his pocket said. He had a mean-looking dragon tattoo that curled out from under the short sleeve of his green mover's uniform and down his huge arm.

Dave stopped and yelled at the other two men, "Hey, let's get these old raggedy chairs off the porch next. Be careful. It looks like they're about to fall apart."

"They are *not* raggedy, and they're not going to fall apart!" Isabel yelled at Dave. "Those are

the best chairs in the world. We sit in them every day. That one is mine."

"Whatever you say, little sister," Dave said.

"I'm *not* your little sister either. I'm *his* little sister," Isabel growled. She pointed her finger at Richard.

Richard gulped and felt the blood rush to his face. He looked around for a place to hide. Dave just stood there staring at him with his big hands on his hips. Richard could see the dragon's tail twitching as Dave flexed his muscles. He couldn't breathe. He couldn't move, either, but he wanted to tape Isabel's mouth shut before she could say anything else to get Dave mad at him.

"That your brother?" Dave said to her.

"Yes. His name is Richard and he's ten whole years old." Isabel put her hands on her hips.

"How old are you, sister?" Dave said.

"Ssssssix," Isabel hissed.

"You're pretty tough for a six-year-old." Dave was looking down at Isabel. Then he looked up at Richard again. "Listen, Richard, man, sorry we got to take these chairs away, but that's the orders." Dave smiled.

Richard breathed again.

"Don't worry about it," Richard said.

"No problem." Dave picked up one of the rocking chairs. "Mr. Hoggle a friend of yours?"

"Yes, sir, he *was*." Richard said.

"He's our best friend," Isabel added. Richard nudged her with his elbow. She had said enough already.

"Well, he sure has some amazing things in there. I've never seen so much junk in my entire life."

"It's not ju . . ." Isabel started to blurt out before Richard clapped his hand over her mouth.

Dave set the chair down somewhere in the back of the truck. The other two men came out of the house. They each grabbed a chair and carried it up the ramp into the truck. The backs of their uniforms were dark with sweat.

"We have to get this stuff out of here today." Dave leaned on the truck's back door and wiped his forehead with a red bandanna. "You kids take it easy."

Isabel looked at the ground and scuffed the toe of her tennis shoe in the dirt.

"I'm going home," Richard said. "Mom will be back soon."

"They took our chairs," Isabel mumbled.

"Yeah, I know." Richard turned his bike around, hopped on, and pedaled out of Hoggle's yard and down the hill as fast as he could.

When he got home, Richard looked back up the street. He could see Isabel still sitting on the curb watching the three movers. He knew she was thinking about the three chairs. And so was he.

CHAPTER 2

▲▲▲▲▲▲▲▲▲▲▲▲▲▲▲▲▲▲▲▲▲▲▲▲▲

Trying to Forget

All Richard and Isabel wanted to do was lie down under the big oak tree behind their house and look up at the green leaves.

Some days they talked about the shapes of the leaves or about how looking up into the tree was like opening your eyes underwater. They had even made plans for building a two-story tree house up in the branches.

But this day was different.

"Hoggle is gone," Isabel said to Richard. She sat up and grabbed a stick and began to draw squiggly lines in the dirt.

"I *know* he's gone. You've said that a hundred times already. We watched the moving truck take all his furniture away yesterday, remember?"

Richard was trying to forget all about Hoggle. Hoggle didn't live on their street anymore and they weren't going to see him again, no matter how much they talked about it.

"I wish you would stop whining, Isabel. We'll just have to find somebody else. That's all."

"But there isn't anybody else."

Richard could see big tears rising up in Isabel's eyes. She rubbed them away with the back of her hand and left a trail of dirt smeared across her cheek.

"Don't cry now. It's no use," Richard said.

To tell the truth, Richard thought he was going to cry himself. He felt like there was a little bird fluttering around in his stomach. He looked away from Isabel and down toward the creek that ran along behind the houses on their side of the street.

"It'll be okay."

"Do you really think that, Richard?"

"Sure," he said, but he wasn't sure at all. He didn't know how it would be without Hoggle.

Isabel kept scratching at the dirt with her

stick, and Richard leaned back against the trunk of the tree and wished for a breeze to come up. And then he wished for a real gust of wind, a tornado, that would come and take Hoggle's house away, just lift it up off the hill where it sat at the end of their street and zoom it to Nebraska or Idaho or Japan somewhere. Then they wouldn't have to look at it, and they wouldn't have to think about all the things that had happened during the spring and summer. Being friends with Hoggle had been like having a bowl of ice cream that never ran out. But, Richard thought, it was all too good to be true. Now he just wanted to forget Hoggle ever existed.

But Richard didn't get his wish. No wind blew. The leaves in the big oak tree didn't even rustle. Sweat kept running into the corners of Richard's eyes. And he kept thinking about Hoggle.

CHAPTER 3

▲▲▲▲▲▲▲▲▲▲▲▲▲▲▲▲▲▲▲▲▲▲▲▲

Rocking Chairs

The first time Richard and Isabel ever sat in the chairs, it was early in March. They had been watching Hoggle since he moved into the neighborhood right after Christmas. Every day he walked from the bus stop to his house that sat at the top of the hill under two huge pecan trees, but they were afraid to talk to him. This particular day, Richard and Isabel were sitting in their driveway with their friends William, Derrick, and Carrie, doing nothing much.

None of them had ever said much to Hoggle before, although he always smiled and said hello or mentioned something about the weather as he passed by. But that day, when he got to Richard and Isabel's house, he stopped and looked at all of them. He had on gold-rimmed glasses. His eyes were gold, too, dark gold like the color of hickory leaves in the fall. His skin was the color of the pecans that fell from the two trees in his yard. He smiled and said, "Well, who's going to come visit me?"

No one spoke. They just shoved their hands farther in their coat pockets and stared at their shoes.

When they looked up again, Hoggle was walking on toward his house.

"My mom says never to go with strangers," William said.

"He's not a stranger, William. We see him almost every day," Derrick chimed in. "My dad talks to him some. He even comes to our church once in awhile. But anyway, he's worse than a stranger. He's a teacher."

"I'm still not going," William said.

"Let's go. I want to go." This was Isabel. She wanted to go everywhere.

"No way," said Carrie, who was a year older than Richard and who liked to give orders more than once in awhile. "There's lots to do right here."

"C'mon, Richard, get up. He's getting away."

"Why should I get up?"

"Because Mom isn't home yet, and she told you to watch me, and I'm going to visit Mr. Hoggle."

Richard shrugged his shoulders. "All I do is baby-sit you." He made his big bad wolf face at Isabel, but she just stuck her tongue out at him. Richard finally gave in. "Okay, let's go if we're going."

"You going to let her boss you around?" Derrick said.

Richard turned and shrugged his shoulders. "Can't help it."

Richard and Isabel walked along behind Hoggle, but Richard made sure they didn't go fast enough to catch up with him.

Hoggle checked his mail and looked up into the pecan trees when he got to his house. Then he went up the sidewalk and sat down in the middle rocking chair. Isabel and Richard stood out in the street.

"He doesn't want us here," Richard said. "He was just trying to fool us."

Hoggle's face was hidden behind the newspaper he was reading.

"This is dumb standing out in the road like this."

Just then Hoggle folded up the newspaper and looked at them. He pointed to the two chairs on either side of him. Isabel ran up the sidewalk and jumped into one of the chairs.

"Wait!" Richard yelled after her, but it was too late. She was rocking away like she had been sitting in that chair all her life. Richard stomped up the steps and sat down on the edge of the other chair. He didn't look at Hoggle.

"Isabel," Hoggle said, "I see the wind blowing in your green eyes. Must be kite-building time."

"How did you know my name?" Isabel's eyebrows almost jumped off her forehead.

"Yeah, how did you know her . . ."

"I know everybody around here, Richard."

Isabel laughed. Richard shut his mouth.

"Are we going to build kites or not?" Hoggle said.

"Please!" Isabel squealed.

Richard shrugged his shoulders and wiped his nose with the back of his coat sleeve.

"Come around back with me, then. We'll have to dig in the storage room some to find what we need."

CHAPTER 4

▲▲▲▲▲▲▲▲▲▲▲▲▲▲▲▲▲▲▲▲▲▲▲

Kite Building

Hoggle's storage room was a little shed painted red like a barn. The door was white and there was a sign painted in green letters on the door. It said:

> *Everything*
> *for Work and Play*
> *Can Be Found*
> *in the Same Place*

Hoggle opened the door to the shed slowly, carefully, like he was afraid something might fall on his head. Richard could hear things sliding and bumping and making little crashes inside the storage room.

When everything finally settled, Hoggle swung the door open wide.

"There," he said, "plenty of stuff to build kites with."

There was enough to build kites with, alright. As far as Richard could tell, there was enough there to build a house with. Hoggle pulled a handful of something from a big box. He handed them each handkerchiefs made of silk and covered with weird designs—trapezoids and hexagons and rhombuses. Richard unfolded one and held it up to the light. The designs started to change. First there were flowers, then fish, then streams and birds, and the cloth flashed blue and green and yellow and silver in the light.

"These are beautiful."

"Thank you, Isabel. My father used to carry one in his pocket every day when he went to work. He gave me a box of them when I moved down here. They make great kite tails, and you have to have a great kite tail if you're going to have a great kite. Right, Richard?"

"Huh? Sure. I guess." Richard was still

watching the fish and birds appear and disappear in the shiny fabric.

Hoggle bent over the box again and started pulling out round wooden sticks and rolls of red and blue paper, bottles of glue and more pieces of cloth. When he stopped, Isabel and Richard both had an armful of kite-making material. Hoggle only carried two huge coils of string.

▲▲▲▲▲▲▲▲▲▲▲▲▲▲▲▲▲▲▲▲▲▲▲▲▲▲▲▲▲▲▲▲▲▲▲

On Hoggle's kitchen table, Richard and Isabel cut and glued and tied string while Hoggle watched and directed them.

When they were finished, Hoggle said, "Richard, your kite reminds me of my favorite bird, a cardinal. All red with a little black around its eyes and a bright yellow beak."

Richard's kite was cut out of red paper, and he had glued two strips of gold cloth across the middle and painted a black stripe between them.

Isabel's kite was made of dark blue paper. She had squirted glue all over it and sprinkled on tons of silver glitter. Hoggle's floor was covered with glitter, too, when she got finished.

"Isabel's kite reminds me of broken glass. It's a mess," Richard said.

"It is not!" Isabel cocked her head to one side and crossed her eyes at him.

25

"Well, it sparkles like broken glass," Hoggle said. "I think it's definitely a Milky Way kite, though. In fact, it's about the best Milky Way kite I have ever seen."

"It doesn't look like a candy bar to me," Richard said. "It doesn't look like anything."

Isabel made her hands into claws and growled at Richard.

"Not that kind of Milky Way. I was thinking of the night sky, maybe in the summer, when you can lie on your back in the grass and look way up into the stars. When there are layers and layers of stars."

"Oh, that Milky Way."

"Yes. That's the one I meant, too, Richard," Isabel said in her little bird voice.

Hoggle laughed. "Time to tie the tails on and get these into the air. The sun will be down if we don't hurry."

CHAPTER 5

▲▲▲▲▲▲▲▲▲▲▲▲▲▲▲▲▲▲▲▲▲▲▲▲▲▲▲▲

Moving the Wind

Hoggle's backyard was big and open, like a meadow, with a tall magnolia tree in the far corner. There was plenty of room there to send up a kite.

"Richard, you go first," Hoggle said. He tested the wind and told Richard to walk to the other side of the yard and run toward him.

Richard took his place on the far side of the yard and started to run as hard as he could. When he felt the wind tug at the kite, he let it go. The kite went up for a moment and then plunged back down, nose first, into the ground.

"Once more," Hoggle said.

"Try again!" Isabel shouted.

This time the wind caught the kite just right, and Richard watched the red bird twitch and turn as it climbed. The handkerchief tail trailed behind like a kaleidoscope snake. Richard backed up slowly until he was standing next to Hoggle.

"Good job, Richard. What a lift-off. Your turn now, Isabel. Show us how it's done."

"This isn't going to work," Richard whispered to Hoggle as Isabel walked across the yard. "She's not old enough."

"Don't bet against it. You just never know." Hoggle winked one golden eye at Richard. "Go, Isabel!" he yelled.

Isabel started across the yard. She ran with short strides and carried the kite behind her. Richard could see the wind tugging at the dark blue paper.

"Let it go!" he screamed. "Let it go now!"

Isabel looked up at Richard and stopped looking where she was going. Her foot caught in the grass and she fell down. Her kite turned on its side and headed straight for the branches of the magnolia tree. Richard started to drop his ball of string and go after her, but Hoggle grabbed his arm.

"She's going to lose it in the tree," Richard said.

"Wait." Hoggle raised his hand and pointed his finger at the kite.

Richard felt the wind come up, and the kite changed direction suddenly, as if someone had steered it out of danger. It rose with the wind up over the power lines and the trees while Isabel's roll of string tumbled across the yard like a runaway Ping-Pong ball.

Isabel got up and ran. She caught the string just before it got tangled in some bushes.

"How did you do that?" Richard said.

"Do what?" Hoggle took his glasses off and wiped them with a white handkerchief.

"You saved her kite. You moved it. I saw you."

"Wind did that. You better let out some string so you can catch up with her."

Richard stared at the kite.

The sun was getting lower now, and the trees turned orange in its glow. Like a flame, his cardinal kite danced in the sunset, sometimes chasing its brilliant tail back and forth at the end of the long string.

As the sun fell farther behind the trees, Isabel's Milky Way kite disappeared against the darkening sky, except for the patches of glitter. They shimmered in the last light of day as her kite took its place among the first stars of night.

▲▲▲▲▲▲▲▲▲▲▲▲▲▲▲▲▲▲▲▲▲▲▲▲▲▲▲▲▲▲

Richard and Isabel were winding the string back on its coils when Derrick, William, and Carrie, along with Mrs. Glover, came around the side of Hoggle's house.

"We saw the kites flying and your mom was looking for you, so we brought her with us," Carrie said. She pushed her blonde hair back over her ears and squinted up at the kites.

"Those are good kites. Where'd you buy them?" Derrick was watching Richard's cardinal flutter back to earth.

"We didn't buy them, we made them," Isabel said.

Mrs. Glover helped Isabel wind in the last length of string. "What a beautiful kite. I have never seen one like this before."

"It's a Milky Way kite, full of stars, Mom."

Mrs. Glover shook hands with Hoggle. "Thanks for looking after the kids, Mr. Hoggle. I hope they weren't a problem."

"No problem at all."

"Richard, your dad will be home any time. Let's get going."

"Can we take the kites with us?" Richard said.

"Sure. Just take care of them. I want to see them fly again."

"Can I carry yours for you, Isabel?" William asked. He was in Isabel's first grade class and tagged along behind her all the time.

"Yes, but go slow."

They all turned and walked toward the road. Richard looked back at Hoggle. Hoggle's golden glasses, or was it his golden eyes, flashed in the dark. "We're coming back, okay?" Richard called.

"I wouldn't bet against it," Hoggle answered.

CHAPTER 6

Nothing But Rain

That spring was full of water. It rained so much the little creek behind the Glovers' house ran over its banks and flooded the backyard.

Richard and Isabel, William and Carrie and Derrick spent the stormy afternoons racing sticks in the gutters or rode their bikes through the pools of water that stood in the streets. Sometimes they sat on Hoggle's porch and watched as the wind swirled in the trees and thunder clouds rushed across the sky scattering lightning as they came.

But, the longer the rainy days went on, the more the children decided just to stay home. Richard, who liked to read, often sat in the big, wing-back chair in his living room with a book about dinosaurs or life on the high seas.

One afternoon, while he was going through the adventures of King Arthur's knights for the second time, Richard heard something strange, or, rather, he didn't hear something. He didn't hear the clatter of the rain against the window or the swish of the wind in the bushes. Everything had gotten still. Richard peeked around the side of the big chair and out the window.

Hoggle was standing at the curb in front of his house holding a huge blue and green striped umbrella. He had on a long gray overcoat, and he stood there, leaning back enough to see the sky from under his umbrella.

Richard jumped up from the chair and got his raincoat off the hook in the hall. He shouted once for Isabel, galloped out the front door, and ran to Hoggle.

It was still drizzling, but there was plenty of room under the umbrella. Richard stood near him and looked up into the clouds where Hoggle was staring. Richard didn't see anything unusual. It looked like the same sky he had

watched almost every day in April and May.

"You think we need all this rain, Richard?" Hoggle said, still looking up into the drizzle.

"No way."

"You think we could spare some then, share it, so to speak, with someone else?"

"They could have all the rain they wanted, if we could send it to them. But we can't."

"Hmmmm," Hoggle said. "Maybe we can. Well, my paper is getting wet. Is Isabel coming?"

Isabel came banging out the front door as if she had just heard her name called.

"Don't leave me."

Hoggle smiled down at her. He twirled the umbrella's stripes once or twice and then started walking toward his house. Richard and Isabel stayed close under the big blue and green dome and tried to keep up.

CHAPTER 7

▲▲▲▲▲▲▲▲▲▲▲▲▲▲

Rain Song

Richard and Isabel followed Hoggle into his living room. Hoggle sat on a little chair near the front door and took his wet shoes off. Isabel and Richard did the same. Hoggle's rugs were soft and deep and they looked like the pictures of flying carpets Richard had seen in a book about Aladdin and the Forty Thieves.

Isabel hopped up on the couch which was draped with a soft quilt patterned with leaves of every color. Richard followed Isabel and sat down. Hoggle took one of the chairs by the small fireplace.

On the wall behind Hoggle was a photograph of a white house with rows of flowers in front of it and three rocking chairs on the porch.

"Those are the same chairs we sit in outside," Hoggle said, "if that's what you're looking at. My grandmama lived with us when I was little. She used to sit in the middle chair between my parents while we children played in the yard."

"What can we do with the rain?" Isabel asked.

"I'm not really sure," Hoggle said. "Richard and I were thinking about sending it somewhere else, where they need rain."

"I feel like a sponge already," Richard said. "My tennis shoes squished all day at school."

"Maybe we could start a big fire outside and dry everything up," Isabel said.

"You can't start fires in the rain." Richard rolled his eyes.

Hoggle rubbed his hands together. "I wonder if drums might work."

"Drums?" Isabel and Richard spoke out at the same time.

"Drums."

"Drums like you hit with drumsticks?"

"Exactly, Richard."

"We are going to get rid of this rain with drums?"

"We can try," Hoggle said. He walked out of the living room and down the hall.

"Are we going to do a rain dance, too?" Richard called after him.

"Shhhhhh!" Isabel put her finger to her mouth. "Be patient."

Richard couldn't stand it when Isabel tried to act like an adult, but he crossed his arms and waited quietly while Hoggle rummaged around in a closet.

Hoggle came back carrying a large cardboard box. He set it down and wiped the dust off the top of the box with his handkerchief.

"Let's see what's in here."

Hoggle brought out two African masks made from thin pieces of wood, painted with bright colors, and decorated with long, white feathers. He gave the larger one to Richard. It had red circles painted around the eyeholes and the mouth was cut straight and serious. The smaller mask he gave to Isabel. Its eyes were surrounded with golden rays, and the little mouth was turned up at the corners, smiling.

Next, Hoggle drew two large wooden blocks from the box. They were hollow and each had

a hole carved in one end. The blocks were painted dark red with a thin white stripe down each side.

Finally, Hoggle took four sticks from the bottom of the box. He gave two to Isabel and two to Richard. The wood they were carved from was jet black and smooth.

"That should do it," Hoggle said as he closed the box and put it up on the couch. "Now, you need to learn a song to play. Put on the masks."

"Are you sure we have to wear masks just to learn a song? Besides, I thought we were going to use drums."

"We are, Richard, but these are special drums."

Richard could see they were special. They didn't look like drums at all, really, more like something Isabel would build a playhouse with.

"They're special because they play the words you have in your mind. If you are angry, the drums speak angry words; if you are happy, happy words come out. If you want to pray, a prayer is what you get. I will teach you a prayer song, a rain song."

"I'm happy," said Isabel.

"That's why I gave you the smiling mask."

Isabel put the mask on.

"I thought we didn't need any more rain," Richard said.

"No, but other folks do. Maybe we can change the direction of some of these clouds."

"Where will the clouds go?" Isabel said.

"Who cares as long as they stop pouring down all over us."

"Africa, maybe," said Hoggle, "but that's not the only place it's too dry."

"We can pray for all dry places."

"That sounds right to me, Isabel. Okay, masks on."

"Where's yours? You can use mine if you want to."

"Thanks, Richard, but I'm not going to play. I can make a mask with my hands while I teach you the song."

Hoggle put his hands over his face and looked out from between his fingers.

"This is how the song goes," Hoggle spoke the words slowly in a soft, low voice:

> Come, gentle rains, come,
> Come nest in the trees,
> Come whisper your song
> To the wheat in the fields.
>
> Come, hard rains, come,
> Come dance in the lake,

Come shout out your song
Until dry grass grows green.

Richard and Isabel listened to the words several times. It was not a hard poem to learn, and it wasn't long before they could say the words back to Hoggle.

"Now that you have the words, you need to learn how to drum. One stick hits loud like thunder; one stick taps soft like rain. These drums lie flat, close to the earth. Try, Richard."

Richard began to play with the two ebony sticks. Isabel watched everything from behind her mask, and Richard was surprised when she started to play right along with him. She didn't miss a beat. Together, they played and played, loud like thunder and soft like rain, while the words of the prayer echoed in Richard's mind.

▲▲▲▲▲▲▲▲▲▲▲▲▲▲▲▲▲▲▲▲▲▲▲▲▲▲▲▲▲▲

Hoggle took their left hands in his. "You've been playing long enough," Hoggle said. To Richard, it seemed like only a moment since they had started. "Supper's probably getting ready at your house."

It was almost dark outside, and the rain had stopped drumming on Hoggle's roof.

Richard and Isabel took off the masks and lay

them in the box, then in went the drums and sticks. They put on their coats while Hoggle walked with them to the door.

Isabel started down the steps and along the sidewalk, but Richard stayed back for a moment.

"You think anybody's going to get this rain besides us?"

"I taught you the song, didn't I?"

"Yeah, but . . ."

"You really played."

"Yes."

"That's as good as you can do. You never know if it will work. Now, go catch your sister. I'll see you soon."

Richard shook his head as he walked down the steps. Was this all a joke? He could hardly believe what he had done. Derrick would have split his sides laughing if he had seen Richard sitting there wearing that ugly mask and banging away on a piece of a log. He was almost sure he would wake up the next day to the sound of rain on his bedroom window.

CHAPTER 8

▲▲▲▲▲▲▲▲▲▲▲▲▲▲▲▲▲▲▲▲▲▲▲▲▲▲▲

A Trip to the Caves

"You did what?" Derrick looked at Richard out of the corner of his eye.

"We sent the rain away. You remember a few weeks ago, the night the rain stopped. That was us, Isabel and Hoggle and me."

"Listen, Richard, I'm your best friend, but this is the goofiest thing I've ever heard."

"How did you send it away?" Carrie asked.

"With drums and African masks and a prayer."

"Did you do a rain dance, too?" Carrie

stomped around in a circle on Hoggle's driveway.

"I know it sounds stupid, but . . ."

"It sounds real stupid, Richard, like something Isabel might say. Nobody can make rain disappear." Derrick crossed his arms on his chest.

"And we let you talk us into going with Hoggle into a cave?" Carrie said. "I thought Hoggle was okay; my mom even said she'd trust him to take me to the moon. She said this trip would be 'educational.' " Carrie rolled her eyes. "After listening to you, I think maybe Hoggle's loony."

"I'm not so sure I want to follow him into some hole in the ground, either," Derrick said.

Richard heard a rumbling sound coming up the street. He turned around as Hoggle pulled a blue and white van into the driveway. The words Museum of Natural History were painted on the front door in red letters. There were dents along the sides of the van, and paint was flaking off around the doors and taillights.

"We're going in this?" Derrick whispered.

"It's kind of beat up," Carrie said. "Looks like somebody swiped a hubcap, too." She pointed at the right front wheel.

"Where are William and Isabel?" Hoggle said

as he came around the back of the van. "Time to get on the road."

"They're in the back exploring the storage room, I think," Richard said.

"Well, you folks find good seats while I go get them."

Carrie ran her fingers along one of the dents. "This thing doesn't look like it could get us to the end of the street, not to mention thirty-five miles to the Cahaba River."

"Listen, I'm sorry I said anything about the drums and the rain. Maybe it was just my imagination. Just drop it and let's have a good time." Richard looked at the dusty seats and the clods of dirt on the floorboard. "It'll be great," he said in a rather weak voice.

▲▲▲▲▲▲▲▲▲▲▲▲▲▲▲▲▲▲▲▲▲▲▲▲▲▲▲▲▲

The ride to the caves wasn't as long as Richard thought it would be. William and Isabel didn't even have time to ask Hoggle, "How long before we get there?"

They followed a paved road that ran next to the Cahaba River for awhile and then turned off onto a gravel trail that headed into the woods. They hadn't gone far on the bumpy gravel path, when Hoggle pulled the van off into a small opening where there was a picnic table and an old garbage can.

Everyone piled out of the van. The sun was up in the sky, but under the tall oak trees there was a cool breeze. Hoggle brought a large box and set it on the picnic table.

"Everyone gets a helmet. Check your lamps and see if they work. It's going to be dark in there."

The helmets were white and each one had a small miner's lamp in front. Richard clicked his on and off a few times.

"Alright, let's go. The cave isn't too far down this path." Hoggle pointed into the thickest part of the woods.

"I wish I was home watching baseball," Derrick hissed.

"Or playing baseball," Carrie added.

CHAPTER 9

▲▲▲

Under the Nevermore Sea

The place where they stopped was completely shaded and the ground was soggy. Hoggle was standing in front of a small opening, like a little door, in the hillside.

"This is it."

"Hmmmmm," Carrie said. "This is juuuuust great."

"Let's go in now," Isabel said.

"Hold it a minute. Remember to keep your lights on and your heads down. It may be a tight fit in there. William, you and Isabel stay close to me."

All three of them bent over and disappeared into the cave.

"Here goes nothing," Richard said.

"I can't believe my mom let me come on this trip," Carrie said as she ducked into the cave. She was taller than Richard or Derrick, and her helmet scraped the rocks as she went in.

"You prayed for that rain to go away," Derrick said. "I sure hope you're praying for us, Richard."

The cave was narrow and damp and dark, although "dark" wasn't really the right word to describe it. *Pitch black* was more like it. The cave seemed to swallow up the little light that came from Richard's lamp. He could hear Isabel chattering away like a bird in front of him, but Derrick and Carrie weren't saying a thing.

Except for Derrick's yellow T-shirt, everything Richard shined his lamp on was gray. There were no gems—no huge quartz crystals or red garnets, no emeralds. As he walked forward, the roof of the cave got lower, and only his helmet saved him from a bad bruise on the head.

Finally Hoggle said, "You can stand up now."

Richard stretched and looked up. They were in a huge room. The ceiling was twice as high as the one in his bedroom.

"There should be some rocks to sit on," Hoggle said. He was sitting in front of the other three and in between William and Isabel. "Rest a little. I want to show you something."

The three older kids found stones and sat facing Hoggle, who was rummaging in his pants' pockets.

"What are you looking for?"

"You'll see in a minute, William."

"I hope it's more exciting than what we've seen so far in this old wet hole."

Richard nodded at Carrie. She was right; this was all very boring, and, besides, he was getting cold.

"Now, everybody turn your lamps off," Hoggle said.

One by one, the lamps went out, and the darkness got thicker and thicker. Richard's eyes hurt.

There was a scratching sound and suddenly the stone room was filled with warm light. A soft red flame flickered at Hoggle's feet.

"Wow!" Derrick almost jumped off his rock.

William and Isabel sat with their mouths open.

Carrie stared at the flame a moment and then looked up. "What are those things on the wall behind you?" she asked Hoggle.

"Seashells. This place used to be underwater, millions of years ago. We're not far from the prehistoric beach."

"Like at the Gulf of Mexico?" William said.

Derrick looked at the wall above Hoggle's head. "This *was* the Gulf of Mexico."

"That's two hundred and fifty miles from here now," Richard added.

"I wonder what it looked like back then," Isabel said.

Then Hoggle spoke again, but this time he didn't sound so much like himself. His voice was distant and soft and slow. In the firelight, he seemed to grow smaller.

Over the rolling waters the wind blew.
There was no sound but the sound the sunlight
makes when it shines on a bright green sea.

No birds circled yet in the skies.
No ships rocked upon the waters.
No human voices sang or laughed or cried.

But the warm sea spoke with the voice
of a thousand lapping waves, and the silent
fish slipped through the shallows.

Hoggle paused a moment and then began again, his voice louder now. Richard felt his eyes closing.

53

And there was a time, now beyond time,
when the big reptiles swam in the warm,
shallow sea. And the blades of their teeth
flashed in the sun. They scattered the huge
schools of fish as they came. The green water
foamed when they twisted and turned,
snapping their great jaws for food.

And then they were gone,
like a dream in the night . . .

For years upon years, there was sunshine
and moonlight, the turn of the tides,
till we came walking these tree-covered shores
to sit in this cave beneath the Nevermore Sea
and watch as the dinosaurs swim in the stone.

Everything was quiet for a minute. No one seemed to breathe. When Richard opened his eyes, he saw that the fire was almost out.

Derrick yawned. "I feel like I've been asleep for a year. But I know I heard every word Hoggle said."

"Me, too." Carrie rubbed her eyes. "But what did he mean by us watching the dinosaurs swim in the stone?"

Richard shrugged.

"Time to turn your lamps back on," Hoggle said. "We're almost out of fire."

"I know what he meant," William said. "Me and Isabel have been watching the dinosaur the whole time."

"There's no dinosaur in here," Richard said.

Isabel pointed high up on the stone wall above Richard's head. Carrie and Richard and Derrick all turned around and looked up. In the last light of the fire, they saw the fossil skeleton.

It stretched across the whole wall of the cave, twenty-five feet or more, from the tip of its tail to the end of its great jaws.

Richard's mouth dropped open and he heard Derrick gasping for air like he'd had his breath knocked out.

Carrie stood stiff as a pole, pointing at the dinosaur's rib cage. "Mama, mama, mama, it's so big," was all she could say.

The group shined their small lights on the huge bones for a long time. Richard tried to imagine the bones coming to life. He wanted to see the dinosaur glide through the prehistoric ocean.

"Okay, Richard," Hoggle said, after a few more minutes. "You lead the way out."

"Richard, I still don't know if I believe you about the rain stuff, but I take back everything I said about coming on this trip," Derrick said as they headed back down the narrow passage.

"That goes for me, too," Carrie added quickly. "This is like our own private museum."

▲▲▲▲▲▲▲▲▲▲▲▲▲▲▲▲▲▲▲▲▲▲▲▲▲▲▲▲▲▲▲▲▲

By the time the van pulled out onto the highway and headed north for Tuscaloosa, William and Isabel were already asleep. Derrick's chin kept dropping to his chest, until he finally slumped sideways and began to snore quietly. Carrie let her arm dangle out of the open window.

Richard leaned his head against the back of the seat and closed his eyes. He imagined himself floating in the warm waters of a long forgotten sea. The gentle waves held him up and rocked him until he drifted into a dreamless sleep.

CHAPTER 10

▲▲▲▲▲▲▲▲▲▲▲▲▲▲▲▲▲▲▲▲▲▲▲▲▲▲▲

An Early Present

It was the day before Thanksgiving, and Richard was still wearing T-shirts to school. It seemed like the hot, dry summer would never end—it might just keep going till Christmas. Decorations had gone up downtown and most of the houses on Richard and Isabel's street had strings of Christmas lights draped along their gutters or wrapped around their mailbox poles. But all the colored paper and pictures of snowmen looked out of place in the heat.

The rest of the summer and most of the fall

had flown by—August had come and Hoggle had moved away. There was a new teacher at the high school, but no new neighbor had moved into the little house at the top of the hill.

School started in September and the summer heat kept beating down on the streets and houses and people. Richard and Isabel looked every day for a letter or a postcard from Hoggle, but none came. They sat under the oak tree in their backyard trying to think of new things to do. At least once each day, Isabel asked Richard if he thought Hoggle would ever come back.

"No," Richard would answer, "he's not coming back. There's no magic around here anymore."

"Do you think he's forgotten us already?"

"Who knows? I don't really care if he has."

"Mama says not to lie, Richard, especially about important things."

"I'm *not* lying. I don't care," Richard would say. "Now stop asking me stupid questions and go away!"

The day after Thanksgiving, Isabel said, "Santa isn't coming."

"What do you mean, 'Santa isn't coming'?" Richard said. "He always comes at Christmas."

"Not this year. It's too hot. He'll burn up in

his wool suit. His reindeer won't be able to fly if it's too warm. I'm not even going to write him a letter."

"Sure you're going to write him a letter. He's bound to come. We've been good kids. He'll make it," Richard said.

"I don't think so." Isabel wiped the sweat off her forehead. "I'm going inside to watch TV."

Richard wasn't sure about Santa and the heat. He was pretty sure he didn't believe in Santa Claus anyway, but he wasn't going to tell Isabel that. Of course, he hadn't believed people could move the wind with their fingers or send a rainstorm away by beating on a drum, either. But that was before Hoggle.

At the moment, though, Richard just didn't care. It was hot under the oak tree, and Christmas seemed far, far away—as faraway as Hoggle was.

"I'm going to get the mail before mom comes home," Richard called to Isabel.

Richard went around the house to the mailbox. He opened it and found nothing inside. He decided watching TV wasn't such a bad idea and started walking toward the front door. Then he saw the mail. But it wasn't letters or magazines. It was a big box leaning against the wall.

The address read,

Richard and Isabel Glover
137 Franklin Terrace
Tuscaloosa, Alabama 35401

and in one corner of the box, in big letters, was the name HOGGLE.

"Isabel, get out here quick," Richard yelled. "Hoggle sent us a box, a big box."

Isabel came running out the front door.

"What box? Where is it?" she asked.

"Right in front of you."

"Is it a Christmas present?"

"I don't think so. It doesn't say anything about Christmas or not opening it."

"Let's take it around back under the tree and open it." Isabel had good ideas every once in awhile.

"You're right, help me carry it."

When Richard and Isabel got the box to the backyard, they set it down and took the tape off. They were sweating and Richard's hands were shaking. Finally, they got the box open. Isabel squealed. There in the bottom, wrapped in newspapers, were the two African masks, the two wooden drums, and the four ebony drumsticks.

CHAPTER 11

▲▲▲▲▲▲▲▲▲▲▲▲▲▲▲▲

Drumming

"We heard something strange," Carrie said, as she came around the side of the house. Derrick was right behind her followed by William. "Richard, is that you?"

Richard took off the African mask. "Yeah, it's me."

Carrie, William, and Derrick stood for a moment staring at the two figures sitting under the oak tree. Then they started laughing.

"Oh, oh, oh," was all Derrick could get out of his mouth. Tears ran down his face he was laughing so hard.

"Where did you get those awful-looking things?" Carrie said.

"They're not awful. They're our masks and drums," Isabel said. "Hoggle sent them to us. He wrote us a note and told us to play our song."

"Hoggle left town three months ago. When are you going to stop talking about him, Isabel?" Derrick said.

"She can talk about whoever she wants," William said.

Derrick ignored William. "What is going on here, Richard? I mean, you can hear those drums all up and down the street."

"Remember me telling you about sending the rain away?"

"That was back in the spring. You aren't still thinking about that crazy stuff?"

"Listen, Derrick, all I know is we played these drums and wore these masks and the rain went away."

"Hoggle says if we play the drums every day, something will come," Isabel added.

"Yeah, the people from the crazy hospital will come and get you and take you away," Carrie said.

William stuck his nose up in the air. "They're not crazy, Carrie."

"We'll see about that," Derrick said. "I'll bet

your parents are going to freak out all over the place, Richard."

Richard sat looking at the drumsticks in his sweaty hands. "I guess they'll just have to freak out then because I'm going to sit here and drum every afternoon."

"You really have gone off the deep end, Richard," Carrie said. "I liked Hoggle fine, and the cave and all the other stuff was neat, but I wouldn't sit out in the heat with those masks on and beat on a log just because he wrote me a note."

"Thanks for the speech," Richard said. "Now if you want to stay and help us, you can. Otherwise, we've got work to do."

Isabel, who hadn't taken off her mask, turned its smiling face toward Richard.

"That's not a hard choice. I'm out of here," said Derrick.

"Right behind you. We can go shoot some basketball at my house," Carrie said. "You coming, William?"

"No." William folded his arms across his chest and leaned back against the trunk of the tree. "I'm staying right here."

"Three goofballs, look at that. Let's get out of here, Carrie."

Derrick and Carrie disappeared around the

house, mumbling to each other as they went.

"You want to see the note Hoggle sent us, William?" Isabel said.

"Sure," said William. "Can I read it?"

"If you promise not to tear it."

"I promise."

Isabel handed William the note, and he held it like it was a piece of his grandmother's china.

" 'Play the drums every day. Something you don't see very often will come. Hoggle.' That's all it says?"

"Yes, William, that's all it says. Isn't it great? Hoggle is coming back," Isabel said.

"Hold it a minute, Isabel. It says *something*, not *someone*, will come," Richard said.

"Sometimes you're just an old lump of mud, Richard," Isabel said.

William giggled.

"Whatever you say, but let's start drumming. I'm getting hot behind this mask. Teach William the rhythm, too, if he's going to hang around."

Soon Isabel and William were taking turns with one of the drums, while Richard played loud like thunder and soft like rain with his ebony sticks. Sometimes when Richard's mind wandered and he missed a beat, he muttered to himself, "This better work. This better work."

CHAPTER 12

▲▲▲▲▲▲▲▲▲▲▲▲▲▲▲▲▲▲▲▲▲▲▲▲▲▲▲▲▲▲▲▲▲▲▲▲▲▲▲

Waiting, Waiting, Waiting

School finally let out for the Christmas holidays. Richard and Isabel played the drums every afternoon, but Richard was starting to worry. Nothing had come, nothing had changed, not even the weather—especially not the weather. It was still warm. Richard wore his Michael Jordan T-shirt and drummed as hard as he could. Sweat popped out on his arms, and the mask started to itch every time he played.

William came most days and helped Isabel.

Derrick and Carrie even showed up once or twice. Derrick took a turn with Richard's sticks, but Carrie only sat on the back steps and shook her head.

"I'm glad I'm not spending the week before Christmas knocking on wood."

"Yeah, but you're here watching us," Richard said.

"That's so I can tell everybody at school what a bunch of jerks you guys are."

Isabel stuck her tongue out at Carrie through the little mouth cut in her mask.

After awhile, Derrick said, "I'm tired. This drum thing isn't working. Nothing's happening. Besides, Hoggle is still gone. I'm leaving."

"At least you gave it a try," Richard said. "Thanks."

"It's still pretty stupid looking," Derrick said. "You aren't going to come out here to-morrow, are you?"

"Nobody, not even Richard, is crazy enough to dress up like a goon and bang on a drum on Christmas Eve," Carrie said as she turned to go.

"I hope not," Derrick added as he followed her.

"I'm glad they're gone," Isabel said.

"I'm just tired. We've been out here every day since Thanksgiving," Richard said. "This is a bunch of junk. At least we could play a different song."

"No," Isabel said. "This is the only song we need to play. That's all Hoggle said to do. Hoggle is coming back, and he is bringing us something, something we don't know about."

"Right," Richard said. "Sure he is."

"It's true," William chimed in.

"Okay. Okay. I'll drum tomorrow if it will make you happy. But we're going to look silly, just like Derrick said, out here on Christmas Eve."

"Something's coming," Isabel said again.

Richard knew she was smiling behind her mask.

▲▲▲▲▲▲▲▲▲▲▲▲▲▲▲▲▲▲▲▲▲▲▲▲▲▲▲▲▲▲▲▲

On Christmas Eve it was seventy degrees. Not warm enough for swimming, but not cold enough for Christmas. Richard and Isabel played the drums that afternoon then ate supper and got ready for bed.

"I hope Santa answers my letter," Isabel said before she went into her room.

"I thought you said you weren't going to write him a letter."

"That was before the box from Hoggle came."

Isabel closed her door, and Richard went to his room to bed.

CHAPTER 13

▲▲▲▲▲▲▲▲▲▲▲▲▲▲▲▲▲▲▲▲▲▲▲▲▲▲▲▲▲▲

Hoggle's Christmas

When Richard got out of bed Christmas morning, something strange happened. His bare feet touched the floor. It was cold, very cold. Richard pulled his socks on and headed for the living room to see what was under the Christmas tree.

It was chilly in the hallway, and Richard had to go back and get his bathrobe out of the closet.

When he got to the living room, no one was there.

"Hey, where is everybody?" he yelled. "Let's have Christmas."

"We're out here! Come see!" It was Isabel. She was standing on the front steps with Mr. and Mrs. Glover.

Richard went to the front door, and he was almost blinded. Everything was so white. After he rubbed his eyes, he saw why.

Snow. There was snow everywhere. The tops of the houses were covered. The limbs of the trees looked like long, slender arms all dressed in fluffy white shirts.

Richard stood in the front door, breathing smoke out of his mouth. He couldn't believe it.

"Something came, something we don't see very often," Isabel squealed.

"Very often? I've *never* seen this much snow, except on TV," Richard said. "It looks like a new world."

People were coming out of their houses all up and down the street. They stood staring at the snow. Derrick's dad kicked at the snow with his house shoes and smiled around the big pipe he held in his teeth.

"It wasn't a rain song we were playing every day after all—it was a snow song," Isabel said.

"I haven't seen snow this deep in twenty years, and never on Christmas," Mr. Glover said. He blew into his cupped hands to keep them

warm. "It's cold out here. You two want to go in and open presents?"

"I think this is our present," Richard said, pointing at the snow.

Isabel winked at Richard. "Hoggle sent it to us."

"Mr. Hoggle sent this snow down here?" Mrs. Glover said.

"Well, we sort of called it ourselves, only we didn't know what we were doing," Richard answered. "That's what the drums were for."

"I don't know if I believe that, Richard," Mr. Glover said.

Just then Carrie came shuffling through the snow. She had on her winter coat, her boots, and gloves.

"You did it! You did it! You brought the snow! Those crazy masks and drums worked!" she yelled.

A moment later Derrick arrived. He was still putting on his jacket. His baseball cap was pulled tight down over his ears.

"Hoggle's note was right," he said. "Something did come."

Mrs. Glover looked at Mr. Glover. "Looks like everyone else here believes Richard's story."

"What do we do first?" Derrick said. His eyes were wide and he was breathing hard like he'd just finished a race.

"Look." Isabel pointed up the street.

Near the top of the hill, they saw William. He was dragging a piece of cardboard behind him. When he got to the top, he put the cardboard down on the snowy street and flopped down on top of it. He came flying down the hill like a penguin scooting across the ice. He stopped near Richard and Isabel's driveway. His face was covered with snow.

"I think we get our clothes on and then find some old boxes to tear apart," Richard said.

"Where did you learn to do that, William?" Isabel said, as William walked up the snow-covered sidewalk.

"I was at Hoggle's house one day in the summer, and we were trying to think of things to keep us cool. He showed me how to make a sled then. He said you never can tell when a cardboard box will come in handy."

In an instant, Richard and Isabel were dressed for the weather and up the little hill in front of Hoggle's old house. They each had a piece of a refrigerator box Derrick's father had saved in his garage.

"I wish Hoggle could see us," Isabel said when she had climbed the hill after her first ride. "Santa didn't answer my letter."

"Yeah, I'd like to see Hoggle take a turn sliding," Richard said as he patted Isabel on the back. "Besides, we still have the drums. Maybe you can make up a new song and bring Hoggle back again."

"Maybe. But I think Hoggle will just come back when he can."

"Your turn, Isabel!" Carrie yelled from the bottom of the hill. "Derrick set the record! He slid all the way to his mailbox!"

"I'll give you a push," Richard said.

"Okay, I'm ready." Isabel sat down on her piece of cardboard, and Richard gave her a good start, then he stood up and watched her fly down the white hill like someone on a magic carpet.

The snow had begun to fall again, and the houses seemed to be wrapped in a swirling, white curtain. Derrick and Carrie and William and Isabel stood in the middle of the frozen street with their faces turned up to the feathery sky. Richard looked back at Hoggle's front porch. In a window, he thought he saw a golden spark, like the light that shone from Hoggle's eyes when he smiled. Richard laughed. "Thank you!" he shouted to the cold Christmas wind and the tumbling snowflakes. Then he jumped on his cardboard sled and was gone down the hill in a flash.